Stop Crying

Renee Miller

Copyright 2016 Renee Miller

This is a work of fiction. Names, characters, businesses, places, events and incidents are either the products of the author's imagination or used in a fictitious manner. Any resemblance to actual persons, living or dead, or actual events is coincidental.

ONE

"Stop crying," Jonas ordered. Although the sound of a woman's misery usually made him hard, the bitch under him sounded like a wounded cat.

The woman, a bottle blonde with jiggly thighs and sagging tits, sniffled. "You're hurting me."

Jonas regretted his choice for possibly the tenth time in the hour since they arrived at the hotel. He selected her because she resembled Annie in the dim light of the bar. Both had blonde hair and big tits, but he quickly found that was where the similarities ended. She lacked the air of superiority his stepdaughter carried, the quiet dignity Jonas had never been able to break.

"You've got snot on your lip," he told the woman. "Annie would never cry like that."

She turned her head, wiping the snot from her mouth onto her arm. "You said you wanted a rape fantasy. Rape victims cry. I was making it authentic and shit."

He let out a calming breath and then rolled off her plump body. "This isn't working."

"Come on, sugar." She smiled, displaying yellow teeth. "I'll do it right this time. Untie me and you can even knock me around a little. Does Annie let you get rough?"

Jonas smiled. "I don't ask for permission."

He walked to the scarred dresser where he'd left his duffel bag. Pulling back the zipper, Jonas felt a tremor in his hands. The anticipation of what came next was almost better than the sex, but he'd promised himself no more mistakes. He'd be careful. No matter what happened, Jonas had to maintain control.

Of course, he also promised to stop thinking about Annie. She'd bewitched him, though, from the second her mother introduced them. Annie was an evil he had to purge from his soul.

And if this bitch didn't play the game right, how was he supposed to be satisfied with anything but the real thing?

"What are you doing?" the woman asked.

"Change of plans." Jonas said. He took a roll of duct tape and a small knife from the bag and then returned to the bed.

The woman eyed the tape and the knife. "I think you're taking this rape thing a little too far."

Jonas tore off a piece of tape. He leaned over her head, but she turned away. He reached for her mouth, but she bit his hand.

"Ow," he said, but chuckled. "Now that's more like it. If only you'd thought of it an hour ago."

He yanked her face toward him and then slapped the tape over her mouth. Her eyes were wide as he held the knife to her cheek. Jonas pressed the blade into her skin, watching her blood trickle over the shiny steel before it slipped down her face. He leaned forward and gently licked it away.

She squealed, but the tape muffled the sound. Jonas grinned and placed the knife on her breast. He dug the tip of the blade into her flesh, and then dragged it around the edge of her nipple.

She jumped, pulling at the ropes that held her hands to the bed. Jonas finished cutting around her nipple and flicked the blade. The once rosy circle of flesh hung from her breast. He looked at her face. Black tears streamed down her cheeks. He'd figured most women use waterproof mascara these days, but liked the dramatic effect. He also liked the way her brown eyes begged him for mercy. The naked fear in her gaze might have been enough for him when they arrived at the motel, but he needed to hear the words now.

"Now," he put the knife to her throat and straddled her thighs. "I'm going to fuck you and you're not going to like it. When I remove the tape, you won't scream, you won't blubber like an idiot, but you *will* fight me as if your life depends on it."

She nodded.

"Because let's be real here," he said. "You're probably not going to survive this. If you say anything that isn't a plea for your life, I'll fuck you with this knife and we'll be done sooner rather than later. Got it?"

She sobbed.

"Pardon?"

She nodded.

"Good." Jonas parted her thighs and slid his dick inside her. She grunted and attempted to wriggle away like a good girl. Annie would struggle like that. He pushed into her hard, forcing her head against the headboard.

She grunted.

"Want me to stop?"

The woman pulled at the ropes around her wrists.

Jonas ripped the tape off her mouth. She gasped.

"What did you say?" he asked, pushing into her again.

"Stop."

"Beg me."

"Please, stop. It hurts. I'll… I'll tell Mother."

Jonas closed his eyes. Fucking idiot.

"Too bad Mother is dead." He said.

She blinked.

"Beg for your life."

She said nothing.

Jonas thrust into her twice more, but lost his erection.

"Fuck." No matter how hard he tried, how good the whore he paid played the role, it was never the same as the real thing.

Jonas slid out of her pussy. He slipped the knife between them, and covered her mouth with his other hand.

The woman screamed as he pushed the blade inside her.

Jonas' erection returned.

TWO

Anna had promised she'd never come back, but her mother's death changed things. She knew her mother hid money in the small box at the back of her closet. If Anna could retrieve it before Jonas got home, he'd never know she was there. She tried to ignore the voice that said no one left Jonas until he decided they could go.

As she walked up the stone steps of the porch, Anna remembered the last time she'd seen him. Five years before, Anna had come home for Christmas break. As soon as she laid eyes on Jonas, Anna became the meek sixteen-year-old who wanted nothing but his approval. She avoided him until her mother went to bed.

"Anna, you look well." He'd said. Jonas was several years younger than Anna's mother, and only eight years older than Anna. She'd often wondered why he married an older woman, when he was attractive enough to have any woman he wanted.

"Thanks," Anna kept her head down. She remembered playing with the button on her dress, tracing the smooth edge over and over again.

"I've missed you."

Anna knew Jonas believed he loved her, but loving fathers didn't have sex with their daughters, or take pictures of them doing unspeakable acts with their toys.

And good girls didn't enjoy it.

"Sit," he ordered. "Have you been eating?"

Anna sat on the sofa, the obedience an instinct she wished she could fight. "I'm fine."

"I worry about you."

"I'm an adult, Jonas. You don't have to think about me anymore."

"You think you're too good for me. Fancy college girl getting fucked by fraternity studs now. Can they give you what you need, Annie? I don't think so. You need a real man; someone who can hurt you in all the right ways."

"I'm not—"

"You think they love you like I do? You think they care about anything but a pretty face and a wet pussy?"

"No," Anna risked a glance at him.

He smiled, but his eyes were cold. "I don't believe you."

"I'm not sleeping with anyone." She lied. Anna had made the rounds of an entire fraternity, but none of them made her feel like Jonas did. He'd broken her.

Anna swallowed. She stood, intent on leaving. "I'll just get my things and be out of your hair."

"I said sit."

Anna didn't sit, but she didn't run. She should've ran.

Jonas stood. He walked the few steps that separated them. "I didn't think your tits could get bigger, but damn, there they are."

Jonas grabbed Anna's arms. He pushed her against the wall. Anna's heart pounded as he fumbled with his belt buckle. "Lift your skirt and turn around."

"I told you we can't do this anymore."

"Shut up." He forced her to turn around, and then pressed her face into the wood paneling with one hand, while the other lifted her skirt.

"Mom will hear us."

"Just one more time." Jonas had whispered.

"I said it was over."

"You came to me, remember? I would've left you alone. Your problem is you think you're special, Annie. You think the world revolves around you and your needs, but you're wrong."

Anna had fought, but his grip was like steel. She felt his tongue on her cheek and though she wanted to resist, the urge to submit was stronger. While she knew she shouldn't, Anna wanted the pain. She needed it.

"Please," she whispered. "We have to stop doing this."

"Fight me, Annie, just like you used to."

"I'm not a kid anymore."

"No?"

"You can't treat me like a possession."

"I think my girl needs to remember her place." Jonas said.

Anna remembered the sting of leather across her backside, and the thrill it elicited between her thighs. She shook the memory of that night from her mind and put a foot on the porch step. Jonas might not have raped her that night, but he had always been cruel. At some point, she started to crave their encounters; required them as much as she needed to breathe. She was just as horrible as Jonas for allowing any of it to happen.

When she'd returned to school, Anna promised herself she'd stay away. Yet, here she was.

Another step, and then one more. Her instincts said to run, but Anna forced her feet to move. She needed the money. Jonas wouldn't give it to her without asking for something in return. One more step and she stood on the welcome mat. She'd made sure Jonas' car was gone, but a sense of dread still hung around her shoulders as she put her hand on the doorknob. Anna inserted the key she'd kept from her last visit and then turned the lock. Taking a deep breath, she glanced at the street one last time before going inside.

THREE

The hooker died almost too quickly. Jonas jerked himself off as she took her last breaths. He'd have preferred to ejaculate in her mouth, but that would ensure he got caught, so he'd left the condom on until he was through. Then he'd taken it off, knotted the end and put it in his pocket. He spent hours cleaning the motel room, and quietly slipped away as the sun rose.

If he could just exorcise Anna from his mind, maybe other women could satisfy him. Maybe not. His father once said all women were whores. They enticed a man, teased him, and pretended to be so fragile and hurt when he took what they offered. He'd believed Anna was different, but after filling Jonas' dreams with her scent, allowing him inside her, begging for more, even watching videos with him, masturbating for him as she watched what he did to other girls, she said Jonas wasn't allowed to touch her anymore. She was a grown woman. Too old for Daddy's hands.

Well, Jonas wasn't her daddy.

As he walked up the steps to his door, Jonas noticed a light in the living room window. He never left lights on. Frowning, Jonas turned the doorknob. He never left the door unlocked either. Jonas smiled as he pushed the door open. He entered the house silently.

The kitchen light was off, so he walked down the hall toward the living room. As he approached the doorway, he heard someone's footsteps on the stairs. Jonas set his bag on the floor and crept back to the foyer. He slipped behind the coat rack and checked his pocket for the knife.

The footsteps were close now. Jonas palmed the knife and waited. A shadow, and then a pale arm reaching for the door. He smiled as he saw the flash of blonde hair.

"I thought you were never coming back," he said.

Anna froze. She turned, blue eyes wide when he stepped from the shadows. "Jonas… I was just—"

"Collecting your money." He found his wife's shoebox the night he killed her. "Did you get it?"

"No." She kept her hand on the doorknob. "But you probably knew that."

Jonas did. He took a step closer, tightening his grip on the knife. "I think you missed me."

She laughed. "Hardly."

"If you'd just stop pretending to hate me, Annie, it wouldn't have been so bad the last time." Jonas took another step. "I was clear on the rules. You give me what I want, and I give you what you want."

"I followed the rules."

"Did you? I recall chasing after you like a desperate puppy. You let me have a morsel of affection here and there to make sure I was never quite satisfied. Clever girl."

"That's not what happened."

"You allowed me to think I'd won, and then you abandoned me."

"What?"

Jonas was hard again, and this time he knew it wouldn't go away. "Don't play the innocent with me. You were happy with me until you went to college. What is it? Decided you could do better? How many have there been?"

She turned the knob, but Jonas covered her hand with his. "Jonas—"

"Five? Ten?"

"How many what? Let me go, Jonas."

"How many men have you used since you left me?"

"None." She said.

She was a lying bitch. He saw the way her cheeks blushed when he grabbed her hand. This was her game. Anna was a succubus. If a man didn't dominate her, she'd suck the life force from him.

"I'm leaving," she said.

"And you'll make another woman pay for your mistakes."

"What are you talking about?"

"I killed someone tonight."

"You're lying."

Jonas lifted the knife. He glanced at the blade, still sticky with the hooker's blood. "Am I?"

"Goodbye, Jonas."

"I don't think so," Jonas walked toward her, forcing Anna to back away. He led her to the sofa. "All this time, I thought I was in control, but we both know that's a lie. It's been you pulling my strings. I tortured myself for years; wanting you, hating myself for it. Sometimes I hated you for giving it to me."

"You should never have touched me."

"And you begged for more. You know, I'd have done anything for you."

"What you did to me was cruel and sick. You made me into a monster just like you."

"I'm tired of talking." Jonas said. He licked the knife blade. The blood tasted stale. Tainted. "We can kiss and make up, or you can try to leave and force my hand. It's your choice."

Anna glanced at the door and then back to Jonas.

He took a few steps, forcing her to back away until her legs met the sofa's armrest. Jonas kept walking until his crotch touched her hip.

"Run, Annie," he whispered as he trailed a finger down her shirt to the waistband of her jeans. "I do love the chase."

She tried to slide out from under him, but Jonas grabbed the front of her pants and yanked her forward. Anna pushed at his chest. Jonas chuckled. He put the knife to her neck and her struggles stopped.

"Jonas, you're better than this." She said.

"I know," he said. "I've learned so many new ways to make you scream. You'll love it."

"I'm your daughter."

"Stepdaughter."

"It's the same thing."

"Not quite."

"Please let me go."

Jonas trailed the knife down her t-shirt. The soft cotton clung to her body, outlining the generous swell of her tits. He remembered the last time he'd fucked her. The way she'd pushed her tits into his hands. She let him hold them the whole time. God, he'd longed to suckle the taut nipples, to make her scream when he bit the tender flesh, but she fought too hard. He'd tortured himself by the weight of her breast in his palm, while he fucked her too quickly.

Jonas pulled Anna's t-shirt from her body and jerked the knife down the front. Anna gasped as the material fell away. He cupped a lace-clad breast that heaved with each breath. She wanted him just as much as he wanted her. Why else would her nipples be so hard. He felt them through the bra, begging for his mouth.

"Jonas—" her voice broke.

His control snapped and he slapped her hard. "You're not supposed to cry."

She bit her lip. Jonas saw a drop of blood at the corner of her mouth, and his cock hardened painfully. He licked the blood away, closing his eyes as he savored the sweetness.

"I want to show you something." Jonas grabbed her hair and then dragged her toward the stairs.

*

Anna stumbled after Jonas, his hand like a vice in her hair. As they reached the top of the stairs, he let go. Anna stumbled into the dark bedroom that used to belong to her mother. She'd barely regained her footing when he turned on the light. She blinked. "What the hell?"

"Nice, right?" Jonas walked toward her. "With you gone and your mother dead, I had to find other girls to take care of me. They just weren't the same, though. No one could live up to my sweet Annie."

Anna stared at the pulleys and ropes fastened to the ceiling. The wall that once housed her mother's bookcase now displayed various whips, restraints and sex toys. Part of her recoiled at what she imagined him doing in this room. Part of her was jealous it wasn't her he was doing it to. God, he was like an addiction.

"Just let me go and I won't tell anyone about this." She promised.

Jonas laughed. "You won't tell anyone anyway, because you want this, Annie. Look at you. Your face is flushed. I bet your panties are soaking wet."

Shame made her look away. He was right. "I won't do this without a fight."

"Promise?" He picked up a leather belt from the dresser, but set it down again. "It's more exciting if there's a chance you'll escape."

Anna looked to the door. Jonas blocked her path. She could try to run, but he'd chase her. When he caught her, she'd be punished. Their sick game would draw her back in and Anna would never break free of him. If she just let him do this, he might let her leave, but would he turn up again and again?

"Weighing your options?" Jonas asked.

"Do what you want." It was clear he expected a fight, so Anna wouldn't give him one. Maybe he'd be so disappointed, he'd forget the idea entirely and Anna wouldn't have to be ashamed of what happened.

"Reverse psychology doesn't actually work, Annie." Jonas shoved her toward the center of the room. "Get on the bed."

Anna considered running one last time, but decided meek compliance was the better way to deal with Jonas. He'd get bored and she'd have a better chance at a clean break.

"We could do it in your bed," she suggested. "Remember how Mom never let me go in there? She'd be so mad."

"Do you want to fuck me in my bed?"

"Yes," she lied.

"Then that would defeat the purpose of this exercise." Jonas said. He reached to remove the scraps of her t-shirt.

Anna held her breath as he cut away her bra. Jonas pushed her shoulders. She flopped on the bed. His hands pulled at her pants, but Anna remained perfectly still.

"Fucking bitch," Jonas said. "You won't just lie there."

Anna felt a burning sensation on her hip, and then her leg. She opened her eyes. Jonas had cut the jeans from her body, his knife also slicing into her skin. The wound was superficial, but it bled profusely like a long, jagged papercut. Anna bit her lip. Jonas was testing her, hoping she'd fight or beg him for more.

"I said, you will *not* just lie there."

Anna didn't move. Jonas yanked the denim from her body and then cut away her panties. Naked, Anna shivered, but closed her eyes again. She wouldn't give him anything.

She felt Jonas' hands on her thighs. His fingers pinched as he parted her legs. Despite her vow to remain still, Anna gasped when Jonas shoved something thick and cold inside her. She opened her eyes, crying out when she saw his face only inches from hers. Jonas jammed it inside her again. Anna grunted, but didn't fight him.

"This one always made you squeal." Jonas pulled the weapon out of her. He put it next to her face. "It loosened things up nicely."

Anna stared. A quick glance to her left showed he held a large purple dildo. She remembered it too well. Jonas used it to punish her, and the sight of it elicited a frisson of fear in Anna's chest.

"Fine. If that's how you want it." Jonas tossed the dildo on the floor and turned Anna onto her belly. He yanked her legs to the side so she bent over the bed and then knelt behind her. "Let's see you pretend now."

She felt his cock against her ass. Her body shook as she prepared herself for the inevitable. She'd sworn this would never happen again. Here she was, though, anticipating the pain, almost hoping for it. What the hell was wrong with her?

"Do something," Jonas ordered, shoving his cock against her ass.

"Do what you want so I can go home."

He yanked her hair, forcing her head back. She instinctively braced her body with her hands, lifting herself to stop the pain in her scalp. Something cold touched her throat. The knife. Jonas dragged it from her collarbone down to her breast.

"Know what I did to the last woman who didn't do as she was told?"

"I'm sure you're going to tell me."

"I wanted to rape her."

"I'm shocked."

Jonas pushed the blade just hard enough to pierce her skin. "She fucked it up, like you're doing, so I cut her nipples off and fucked her with the knife."

Anna swallowed the sob that caught in her throat. He didn't. Jonas was messed up, but he wouldn't... she remembered the blood on the knife blade. "It isn't rape if she lets you do it. Why would you punish her for doing what you wanted anyway?"

"Because of you. Her death and the others are your fault."

"I'm not the one who killed them."

"You got under my skin, made me love you, and then suddenly, I wasn't allowed to touch you. I couldn't even talk to you anymore. You just left. Do you know how that twists a man? I had to go to hookers, because your mom said it was the only way. They just weren't the same. When I tried to inspire them, they cried and carried on… I had to shut them up."

"Are you going to kill me?" Part of her welcomed death. At least she'd never have to see Jonas again or face the ugliness he'd created inside her.

"Not if you give me what I want."

"I am." She pushed against him, but Jonas kept the knife at her breast. She felt the sting of the blade as it pierced her nipple. This was new. Jonas could be rough, but he'd never actually hurt her.

"You're giving me nothing." He said. "It wasn't supposed to be like this. I'm supposed to win you. You don't win anything without a fight."

Fine, he wanted a fight, he'd get one. Anna reached for the knife. To her surprise, she managed to grab the blade and yanked it from Jonas' hand. He jumped back as she swung her arm. Anna rolled onto her back, holding the knife in front of her.

Jonas laughed. "That's my girl."

"Last chance," she said, courage filling her with strength. "Let me go or I'll kill you."

"Stab me. Go on. Let's see if you've got the balls to take control."

FOUR

Anna's face was flushed. Jonas let her stand, watched her arm shake as she swayed slightly on unsteady legs. Jonas knew she was bluffing, but she put on a marvelous show. He advanced, his eye on the knife, and she lunged toward him.

Jonas took the knife from Anna with minimal effort, and then grabbed her arms. Forcing them behind her back, he pushed her toward the bed. She fought; bit his arm, but he held her tight. "Come on, Annie. Make it hurt. I'm so hard I could explode right now."

"You're fucking crazy," she spat.

"And you love every second of it." Jonas forced her to bend over the bed again. This time he pulled a whip from the peg on the wall. He looped it around her neck and then pulled back on it. Anna choked, her hands grasping at the whip. "This time, I'm not playing nicely. I plan to give you some souvenirs to take with you."

He forced his hand between her legs. Jonas allowed himself a brief moment to enjoy his victory before shoving three fingers inside her. He bent them slightly. Women loved this move. He felt Annie's muscles clench, and she gasped. "You like that?"

She shook her head, still clawing at the leather around her throat.

"Liar," he rubbed her clit. "Were you this wet for those college boys?"

"Stop," she rasped.

Jonas considered fucking her the old-fashioned way, but she expected that, and who knew how many men had already been there. He parted the cheeks of her ass. She tensed reflexively and he smiled. Pulling the whip tighter, Jonas forced two fingers into her ass. "I'm going to make you bleed," he promised.

She choked. "Can't breathe."

Jonas loosened his hold on the whip. She gasped for air. He allowed her a second of relief, and then pushed his cock in her ass, eliciting a curse from her usually sweet lips.

"That's it," he said. "Clench it tighter."

Anna cried, pushing against him.

A roaring in his ears silenced Anna's gasps. Something snapped inside Jonas, a thin thread he'd always kept taut, but never broke. Somewhere outside his body, he heard Anna scream. He tasted blood, heard the strangled sounds of her cries, and then his orgasm obliterated everything but the rush of pleasure in his balls.

Jonas rolled Anna onto her back. He wrapped the whip around her wrists and then dug the knife into her breast.

*

Anna clutched the steering wheel. She didn't know how long she drove, or in what direction, but suddenly she couldn't stop the tremors wracking her body and she pulled the car over.

She sat on the side of the road, car turned off, staring at her bloody hands. Her ass throbbed. Her neck felt as though it was on fire. The rough wool of the coat she'd taken off the back of the door as she ran from the house rubbed against the wounds his teeth left on her back and her shoulders. She knew she was bruised and bloody, but Anna couldn't go to a hospital.

If she told on Jonas, the cops would arrest him. Jonas was a smooth talker, and he'd convince them their relationship was consensual. Anna let out a frustrated sigh. He'd be right. Until last night, she'd enjoyed fucking him. Until last night, he wasn't a fucking lunatic. She'd just have to figure out a way to get rid of Jonas herself.

The sky had darkened considerably since she left her childhood home. Streaks of pink and purple painted the horizon. Tomorrow would be a nice day. Anna remembered staring at many similar sunsets, hoping she'd wake up and be normal and find a normal guy to have normal kids with.

Instead she'd wake up thinking about Jonas.

A tap on her window startled Anna. She glanced to her left. A woman with dark red hair and a kind smile stared back. Anna turned the key in the ignition and then pushed the button to lower the window.

"Are you okay?" the woman asked.

"I… no."

"What happened, honey?"

"Nothing. I'm okay."

"You're bleeding."

"I'll be fine." Maybe if she said it enough, she really would be okay.

"Listen," the woman leaned on the side of the car. "You don't have to tell me what happened, but those wounds need to be cleaned up. Follow me home and I'll look after you. If you still don't want to call the police, that's fine. I won't make you do anything you don't want to do."

"Don't worry about it. I'm fine."

"He can't hurt you now."

Anna frowned. How did she know?

"Whoever he is," the woman continued, "he's not here and he doesn't have to know you told someone. Sometimes it's just easier to let it all out."

Anna nodded. "It was my stepfather."

The woman scowled. "You okay to drive?"

"I think so."

"You know what? Let's leave my car here. I can send a friend to pick it up. I'll drive you to my place. You can leave any time you want to. Okay?"

Anna stared.

"Miss?"

"Anna."

The woman touched Anna's arm. "Anna, it's all right. You're safe now."

"I am."

"Scoot over and I'll take care of you."

*

Jonas let Anna leave. He was too happy to chase after her. She'd never tell a soul anyway. He owned her now. If he wanted her again, he just had to find her. He knew it, but more importantly, Anna knew it.

Maybe he'd finally find peace. Anna was finally his and everything was right with the world.

He rolled onto his side and pulled the nightstand drawer open. Jonas picked up the remote and then aimed it at the television on the wall above the dresser. He pressed "play" and the bedroom appeared on the screen. Anna stumbled in. Jonas strode into the frame a moment later. He smiled as he watched, his cock hardening. Circling the tip with his fingers, Jonas skipped to the part he remembered only vaguely. He paused the video, capturing a moment of pure terror and agony on Anna's face. He stood behind her, cock in her ass, knife sliding across her chest. The blood froze on the screen, tiny droplets caught in midair as it dripped from the knife to the bed. Anna's eyes were wide, her teeth bared.

Jonas gripped his cock and stroked the blanket with his other hand. He looked down. Anna's blood feathered out across the satin, like an ink stain. It was still wet. He rolled over on his belly, pressed play and then turned up the volume. Rubbing his cock against Anna's blood, he listened to her scream.

He slid up and down the moist stain, an orgasm mounting as he listened to the sounds of him finally winning Anna.

FIVE

Anna stayed with the redhead, whose name was Fiona, for several weeks. Fiona opened her home to what she called women in trouble. They'd stitched Anna's breasts and bandaged the torn skin on her back. Most of the wounds had healed, although many would scar, leaving her a permanent reminder of Jonas' power.

Fiona explained she'd taken Anna's car back to the highway and ran it into a pole. Then she'd set it on fire so no one would look for her. As far as the rest of the world knew, Anna was dead. For the first time in years, she felt safe. Fiona was strict, but kind. She was gentle, but firm in her demands of the women in her home. They all pitched in, and they all participated in daily "group" therapy sessions. Anna was silent the first few days, but

Fiona said she couldn't stay if she wasn't willing to start the journey toward healing. So, Anna had shared her story.

At first, Anna feared they'd blame her, but as she told them about Jonas, she saw fury in the eyes of the other women. When they reacted to what she told them, Anna realized they were angry on her behalf.

"He can't get away with that," Julie, a petite brunette whose boss assaulted her multiple times before she went to the police, said. "If we let him go, he'll do it again. He's already killed one woman by his own admission."

"He didn't say the hooker died," Anna reasoned, unwilling to believe Jonas would go quite as far as murder. He was trying to scare her. Fear was part of their attraction.

"He fucked her with a knife," Julie said.

Anna didn't reply. She didn't like Julie very much. In fact, she was getting tired of Fiona too.

"Give Anna time," Fiona said. "You refused to do anything when your rapist got off with a slap on the wrist. Even when they found you bloody and broken for a second time, you scurried around here like a frightened animal, refusing to call the police. How long did it take you to get strong enough to fight back?"

Julie shrugged.

"Okay," Fiona stood. "It's time for Anna's private session."

The other women filed out of the room. Anna stayed in her chair. The room, a sort of office and lounge that had a desk, several comfortable chairs, and a soft daybed, was the nicest in the house. Anna felt safe there. Too safe.

Fiona sat on the chair next to her and touched her arm. Anna jumped, pulling away from the unexpected contact.

Fiona sighed. "I won't hurt you."

Anna found herself wishing Fiona would hurt her. It'd at least break up the monotony of her life at the moment. "Sorry."

"Don't apologize."

"Sor—I'm not used to this." Anna knew Fiona liked her in a way that wasn't platonic. The knowledge made her nervous, but excited.

"Let's try a little exercise." Fiona said. "You touch me."

"What?"

"Touch me. It's time you were in the driver's seat."

Anna laughed. "Sounds silly."

Fiona unbuttoned her blouse. "You're used to being the victim. Today, you're the aggressor."

"I can't hurt you." She remembered Jonas telling her she didn't have the balls to take control.

"I'm not asking you to, although if that's what you want, then it's your call." Fiona took her blouse off. She moved her hands to her bra, removing that as well. "Touch me."

Anna sighed. Fiona guided Anna's hand to her breast. The sensation of skin on skin was like touching a flame to gasoline. Anna felt a twisting in her belly.

"Feel that?" Fiona asked.

Anna nodded.

"My heart is racing because I *want* you to touch me."

Anna felt Fiona's nipple harden under her hand. She squeezed, and heard Fiona's soft intake of breath. "Does that hurt?"

"No," Fiona smiled.

Anna resisted the urge to squeeze harder. "We shouldn't be doing this."

"Part of your recovery requires you to trust your body and its impulses, Anna. Only when you allow yourself to have what you desire, to be in control and take what you want, will you be ready to deal with your stepfather."

The mention of Jonas sobered Anna. She wanted him to suffer as he'd made her suffer, and she knew he was waiting for her with as much certainty as she knew the way her vagina throbbed when Fiona touched her was bad news.

Fiona stood and then pushed her pants down. Anna didn't move a muscle as she slid the pants over her hips, down to her knees, and then kicked them aside.

Fiona parted her thighs. She inserted her fingers into her vagina. She moved them in and out, parting her legs wide enough for Anna to watch. "See how wet I am? That's because of you."

"I…" Anna licked her lips. Fiona thought she controlled everyone in this house. They ate when she said, talked when she decided it was time, and now, Anna was supposed to just lay back and get fucked, because Fiona wanted her to.

"Loving someone isn't wrong." Fiona pulled her fingers from her body and lifted them to Anna's lips. "Just because you have a vagina doesn't mean you're weak."

"I know I'm not weak." And she loved no one.

"Do you? Take what you want then."

Anna smelled the musky scent of Fiona's vagina. She licked the tips of her fingers. Fiona stepped closer. Closing her eyes, Anna took Fiona's entire finger into her mouth.

"Now, what else do you want, Anna?"

Anna opened her eyes. Fiona had moved closer. Her pussy was now only inches from Anna's face.

Fiona sighed. "Touch me. Make me cry, make me scream; whatever you want, I am giving you permission to do it."

Anna licked her lips. Both Fiona and Jonas wanted her to take control. Fine. Anna slid her hand between Fiona's legs. Fiona parted her thighs, but did nothing else. Anna stared at Fiona's labia, fascinated by her hairless body. She lifted her fingers, parted the folds, and then stroked Fiona's clit gently. Fiona gasped, pushing against Anna's fingers. Anna pressed harder, pinching Fiona's clit the way she remembered Jonas doing to hers. The memory brought a sense of shame to Anna's heart.

"Don't stop." Fiona held Anna's hand against her clit.

Anna pinched her clit again and was rewarded with a soft gasp. Anna slid a finger into Fiona's vagina. It felt hot, slick, and she felt the muscles contracting around her finger. She pushed harder.

"Fuck," Fiona whispered. "Put another finger in me. Turn your hand so you can put your thumb in my ass."

Anna obeyed, and then looked up at Fiona's face. Her cheeks were flushed, her mouth open. Anna pushed her fingers in and out of Fiona, spreading them wide and then curling them at the knuckle. Fiona leaned her hips into Anna's hand, grinding against her thumb.

"Harder." Fiona ordered. "Hurt me."

Anna smiled. She curled her fingers into a fist and thrust it inside Fiona.

"Christ," Fiona breathed.

"Do you like that?" Anna asked. Her voice sounded strange.

"Yes. Do you?"

Anna nodded. She pushed her knuckles in and out of Fiona's pussy, marveling at how the other woman became wetter with every thrust. The scent of her body drifted to Anna's nose. Her mouth watered.

"Do you want me to kiss you?" Anna asked.

"It's not about what I want." Fiona said. "Do you want to kiss me?"

"I don't know." Anna lied. She liked being in control.

"Maybe I should kiss you."

"Please," Anna removed her hand. Fiona knelt in front of her. She helped Anna remove her pants, and then kissed her thigh. Fiona rubbed her clit through the thin cotton panties, gently, but with enough force to send jolts of heat through Anna's thighs.

"Any time you want to stop, say the word and it ends." Fiona said.

Anna nodded. She wished Fiona would just get on with it.

"Stand up?"

Anna stood.

Fiona kissed the scars on her stomach. When Anna used to cut herself, she chose places only Jonas saw, because he liked to see the evidence of her pain. Her thighs had the same scars. Thanks to Jonas' recent cruelty, so did her breasts. Fiona gripped Anna's hips and buried her face between her thighs. Anna felt the warmth of Fiona's tongue through her panties, and closed her eyes.

Fiona pulled Anna's panties down. Anna felt the cool air briefly, but Fiona's mouth was on her in a heartbeat. She felt the warmth of Fiona's tongue on her clit as Fiona sucked it into her mouth. Anna gasped.

Fiona sucked again, and Anna saw dots of light in front of her eyes. She ached for something more, though. Fiona licked and sucked until Anna's legs were weak. She put her hand in Fiona's hair, pushing her face closer.

"Bite me." Anna said.

Fiona nipped at her clit. It wasn't enough.

"Can I put my fingers inside you?" Fiona asked. "Like this."

Anna felt Fiona's tongue inside her.

"Yes?"

"Yes."

Fiona pushed her fingers inside Anna, and then resumed teasing her clit with her tongue. Anna's ears roared and she gripped Fiona's hair as though it were a lifeline. She cried out as a wave of heat coursed over her body and the dots of lights exploded behind her eyelids.

"Was that good?" Fiona was still on her knees.

It could've been better. "I guess so."

Fiona laughed. "Now it's your turn."

"I thought that was my turn."

Fiona walked to the desk and opened the large drawer at the bottom. She stood, revealing a dildo attached to a harness. Anna's heart skipped a beat. "Relax, love. This is going inside me, not you."

Anna frowned.

"You'll strap this to your body," Fiona showed her the harness. "I generally don't like these, but you need to do this."

"Why?"

"Because the act will give you back your power."

Anna frowned. She had the power already. Fiona thought she was manipulating the situation. She was calling the shots, after all. Deep inside Anna's head, she felt something give way. Something she'd held in place for far too long. Its absence was freeing.

"You won't be free of Jonas until you take control."

"And how does this help?"

Fiona smiled as she stroked the fake penis. "You'll see. When we're through here, you'll see how we'll deal with that stepfather of yours."

"I'm going to… fuck him?"

"*We're* going to fuck him, but that's not all."

"I want him dead."

"We never let them live."

Anna took the harness, but she didn't put it on. Removing the dildo, she approached Fiona. "I'm in control."

"Good." Fiona bent over the desk. "Fuck me."

Anna smiled. "I'm going to make you scream."

"I hope you do."

Anna took the harness in both hands and then looped it around Fiona's neck.

"What are you doing?" Fiona stood.

Anna pulled the harness tight. Fiona struggling to remove the strap from her neck, the sound of her gasping for air sent a surge of moisture to Anna's pussy. Anna pulled back until Fiona's struggles weakened.

"I'm tired of submitting," Anna said as she wrapped the leather straps around one hand and picked up the dildo with the other. She leaned over Fiona's back, sliding the dildo inside herself. "Is this enough control for you?"

"Please," Fiona's voice was raspy.

Anna appreciated what the women in the house had done for her, but in her own way, Fiona had done just as Jonas had done for years; she'd manipulated Anna. She'd dominated her.

Sliding the dildo in and out of her pussy, Anna watched Fiona struggle for breath. Fiona's eyes closed, and she stopped fighting. Anna released the harness and Fiona slid to the ground. She tossed the dildo aside, another idea forming in her mind.

"I think it's still my turn." Anna said, and straddled Fiona's face. As she ground herself against

Fiona's mouth, the other woman found a little more fight somewhere inside. She scratched Anna's thighs, and then her ass. Anna closed her eyes, marveling at the pressure already present in her pussy. She ground harder, Fiona's muffled screams only adding to her arousal. As she climaxed, Fiona stopped struggling.

SIX

Jonas had spent hours at the police station. The cops found Anna's car on the highway. She'd hit a pole and the car exploded. As her next of kin, he got the call. No body, though. Anna was alive and mostly well when she left that night. It wasn't his fault she drove like an idiot.

They said she probably got thrown from the car, and expected to find her body soon. He felt empty with her gone.

He flicked the switch on the wall, flooding the living room with light. He was startled to see Anna sitting on the sofa.

"Hello, Jonas."

"Annie," he walked around the sofa. "You look well for a dead girl."

"Do I?" She stood as he neared the sofa.

"Not that I'm complaining, but why are you here?" She was too calm. Too… happy.

"We need to talk." She said.

"You're supposed to be dead." He took a step toward her. Anna retreated. She was scared. He liked her scared. "Let's start with that."

"Can we go upstairs?"

Jonas was confused, but also curious. He waved toward the stairs. "You first."

Anna led the way. There was no pause, no moment of uncertainty. She walked up the stairs without looking back to see if he followed. Jonas frowned. This wasn't his Annie.

She walked to his bedroom door and turned. "We don't have to fight each other. This thing we have; it can be good."

He laughed. "I don't want it to be good. Sweet Annie, I like it when you fight me. I need it."

"So, I'll fight if that's what you want, but I prefer you hurt me without drawing blood."

He shook his head and pointed. "If you want this, and I know you do, we do it my way."

She followed his hand. Her smile faltered. "You can't fuck me without tying me up?"

"I didn't tie you up last time."

"You had a whip around my throat. I couldn't do much but beg you to stop."

He nodded. "Good point."

"Maybe you're not man enough to fuck me without the help of restraints."

"I am."

"Prove it."

Jonas didn't like her tone. He'd do whatever he pleased. The cops thought she was dead, so he didn't have to play nicely anymore. He grabbed her arm and then dragged her against his body. She slapped his face. The sting of her palm against his skin shocked him, but Jonas grinned.

"Let go." She demanded.

"Make me."

Annie lifted her knee, but he jumped away.

"So that's how it is?" he asked.

"You won't break me."

He dragged her to the guest bedroom. "I already have. And now that the world thinks you're dead, I can do so much more."

Anna kicked at his shins. While her booted foot elicited fiery shots of pain, Jonas didn't loosen his hold on her arm. He pushed the door open and shoved her inside. Anna tried to push past him, but Jonas shoved her again. He didn't bother with the light. Jonas knew every inch of the room.

He listened to her panting. She wouldn't admit it, but Jonas knew she needed his dominance. Why else would she have come back after the perfect escape?

"I didn't want it to go like this," Anna said.

"It's not about what you want."

"Oh, but it is."

Jonas took a step, but something fell over his head. He felt hands on his arms and struggled, but the click of handcuffs followed, and then a pinch at his neck. Jonas lunged forward, but his head felt heavy. He managed to shove the hands away, but blackness obliterated what happened next.

*

A searing pain ripped through Jonas' belly, dragging him from the blissfulness of sleep. He opened his eyes. At first, he only saw blurred colors. He blinked, and Anna's face appeared in front of him. He tried to move, but realized his hands were bound over his head. He looked up. Anna had cuffed his hands to the harness that hung from the ceiling. He struggled, but it held firm.

"Fucking cunt."

She smiled.

Jonas realized she was naked, but the searing pain in his belly made the fact seem unimportant. He heard a sucking sound and then looked down. Anna guided a long blade across his stomach, lifting and separating a narrow strip of flesh from his body as she did so.

"Fuck!" Jonas screamed. "Have you lost your mind?"

"I thought you liked this," she lifted the knife to his nipple. "Remember how you cut mine? Nipples don't grow back." Anna flicked the blade, slicing his nipple clean off. "Now we're twins."

Jonas screamed. The pain was indescribable. His head swam, but his body was alert. All senses on edge. "You'll regret this. When I get loose—"

"You won't. It's my turn."

"For what?"

Anna smiled as she lifted the purple dildo. "Remember old reliable? You said it was your favorite. Really loosened things up if I recall correctly."

Jonas felt sick. He watched Anna walk past him.

"Annie," he warned. "You're making a mistake."

He felt her hands on his ass. She parted his cheeks, and he jerked as he felt the tip of the dildo in his asshole.

"If you fight me," Anna said. "It'll hurt more."

He bucked as she drove the dildo into his ass. The breath left his lungs when she pulled it out and then thrust it in again. He didn't want to, but Jonas heard himself cry out. Anna didn't stop her assault. He felt her nails bite into his hips as she pushed the dildo into his ass again and again.

"Stop." Jonas begged.

Anna pushed harder. "You're not supposed to cry."

She left the dildo in his ass as she walked to the bed. He watched her pick up a knife. Fear gripped his belly when she put the knife to his penis, which was unconscionably erect.

"Remember how I didn't have the balls to take control?"

"No."

Anna smiled and moved the knife to his remaining nipple. He screamed as she tore the tender piece of flesh from his chest bit by agonizing bit.

"God, I'm so wet." Anna's voice was breathless. "I need you."

She turned around, pressed her ass against his cock and then spread her legs. Jonas shuddered as she put his cock inside her. She let out a long sigh as she guided him in and out.

"When I left here," Anna said, pushing her ass against him. "I was rescued by a woman. She ran a home for abused women."

"You're not abused."

"I have no nipples, Jonas." Her voice was cold.

He gasped as she pushed against him again. God, he was going to cum in a matter of seconds if she didn't stop.

"They were nice women," Anna continued her story. "But so controlling. I couldn't go outside. I had to own my anger. Talk about it. That was the worst part. All the fucking talking."

Jonas felt his legs quiver. Just as his balls tightened, she stepped away.

"And then the woman—her name was Fiona—tried to manipulate me. I was so sick of being someone's submissive. So I did what you told me to."

Jonas felt a sob in his chest. His erection had become painful and he didn't like the way she slid her finger up and down the knife blade. He knew the look in her eyes too well.

"Thanks to those dearly departed ladies, I took control. First, I seduced the woman who rescued me, letting her believe she'd seduced me." Anna smiled. "And then I strangled her with this harness thing she wanted me to fuck her with."

"You didn't." His Annie didn't have a murderous bone in her body.

Anna walked around his body and he felt the dildo forced into his ass again.

"I'll kill you for this," he promised.

"Don't tease, Jonas. I'm already so wet," Anna said. "I could explode."

He didn't want to like what she was doing to him, but damn, he loved it.

Anna released the dildo and walked around his body once more. "But I didn't kill her just then. Just as she hovered between life and death, I sat on her face and suffocated her with my pussy. Did you know it's possible to achieve orgasm simply through the vibrations of another person's screams?"

White hot pain in his thigh tore Jonas' gaze from Anna's cold stare. She slowly cut away a strip of skin on his thigh.

"And then I stole some sedatives from her desk drawer. You sampled some a little while ago. I told the others Fiona went into town and put I made soup for lunch. Once they fell asleep, I set them on fire. No witnesses, right?"

He writhed as she pulled the skin back and then left it dangling. Anna placed the knife closer to his balls and dug the blade deep into his flesh. Jonas screamed again, and then darkness took him once more.

*

"Jonas," Anna said sweetly. "Time to wake up."

He blinked and then opened his eyes. "Annie? You're dead. They said…"

Jonas bucked against the harness, but realized he was still bound and he leveled a steely glare her way. "Let me go and we can talk."

"I don't think so." Anna said.

Jonas felt the knife against his penis. "No. Please, Annie. This isn't you."

Anna sighed. "What's happening to you is your fault. You just couldn't leave me alone."

"If you let me go, we can both enjoy this. I have so much I can teach you."

"I think I've learned all I can from you."

Jonas' penis felt like it was on fire. He looked down, and choked as he watched Anna trail the tip of the knife over his shaft. Blood followed the blade. Vomit burned the back of his throat. She wouldn't cut it off. She couldn't.

"No," he breathed. "Please, Annie."

"Stop crying," she moved the blade to his penis and then sliced the length of his cock again. "You're ruining the mood."

Jonas wailed, but no sound came out.

Anna sliced the underside of his penis. His vision blurred as she peeled the skin back slowly.

"I'll kill you," he managed.

"I'm already dead."

"Please…"

"I'm going to fuck you until you can't stand the thought of fucking anymore." Anna said. "And while I do that, I'm going to peel away every inch of skin on your body."

Jonas stared. Gone was the timid girl he'd dreamed of owning. In her place was something he'd never seen before. She was cold, cruel. Demonic.

"I won't survive that." He said.

Annie grinned. "That's a risk I'm willing to take."

THE END